S0-CSZ-069

Double Ugh
by Anne de Graaf
Illustrated by Evelyn Rivet
© Copyright Scandinavia Publishing House 1992
Published by Scandinavia Publishing House
Nørregade 32, DK–1165, Copenhagen K
Denmark
Text: © Copyright Anne de Graaf 1990
Artwork: © Copyright Evelyn Rivet 1992
Printed in Italy 1996

Published in the United States of America by
Abingdon Press
201 Eighth Avenue South
Nashville, Tennessee 37203

First Abingdon Press Edition 1996
ISBN 0-687-07139-9

TINY TRIUMPHS
DOUBLE UGH

By Anne de Graaf
Illustrated by Evelyn Rivet

Dedicated to Erik

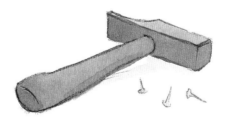

Abingdon Press

One day Mommy was hammering a nail, when she missed.
She yelled a word and shook her thumb.

"That's a new word," Julia looked up from her bike.
"What does it mean?"
"Never mind," Mommy said.
"It's a bad word."

Another day Daddy was trying to fix the washer, when he flooded the basement.

He yelled a different word and threw the wrench on the ground.

"But I *am* sitting," Daniel said from the stairs.
"Never mind," Daddy said.
"It's a bad word."

That's when Daddy and Mommy asked God to help them.

Before long Daniel turned the water on in the tub and let it flood into the hallway.
Before Mommy could say anything,
he said, "Sit!"

"What?" Mommy roared.

"That's what Daddy said when he made a mess,"
Daniel grinned.

"But I know he told you it was a bad word.
So now you have to say it fifty times.
And after that you're not going to say it again.
And after *that*, you're going to clean this up."

Poor Daniel. The first twenty times were fun.
"Sit, sit, sit, sit, sit, sit, sit, sit, sit, sit, sit, sit, sit, sit, sit, sit, sit, sit, sit, sit."

But during the next thirty times,
the word became less and less special.
"Sit, sit, sit, sit, sit, sit, sit, sit, sit, sit, sit, sit, sit, sit, sit, sit, sit, sit, sit, sit, sit, sit, sit, sit, sit, sit, sit, sit, sit, sit."

When Mommy finally told him he could stop,
it was no fun to say anymore.

Before long Julia fell down and yelled.
She used the same bad word Mommy had
used when she hammered her thumb.

"What?" Mommy roared.
Julia said the word again.

"That's terrible.
Little girls shouldn't
say words like that."

Julia slipped her hand
into Mommy's.
"You did."

"Yes, well, I'm not a
little. . . ."
Mommy took a deep
breath.

Julia said, "It's okay, Uncle Bernard says it, too. Only he puts God in front of it."

"No, that's not okay," Mommy said.

"Actually, that's worse. When you say that word with God's name, you're telling God you don't love Him.

You're saying you don't care."

Julia was quiet for a minute. "But what should I say then?"

Now Mommy was quiet for a minute.
"Say ow. Or say ugh.
And say double ugh if it really hurts.
But remember, whoever says a bad
word again has to go to her room for
five minutes. Deal?"

Julia nodded, "Deal."

Later, when Julia caught her finger in a door, she yelled, "Ow!"

Mommy kissed her finger.
"Good girl for not saying a bad word.
Say ow again, as loud as you can."

"OW!"

Mommy laughed, "Now there can't be anymore ow left.
It's such a tiny finger."

"Ow!" Julia whispered.

But when Mommy bumped her head on the cupboard door she said a bad word again.

Julia looked up from her blocks.
Mommy said, "I mean ow."
She rubbed her head.
"I guess I better go to my room, huh?"

Julia said, "It's okay. I'll come with you."

Mommy told Daddy what had happened and that's when they thanked God for helping them.

Now when Mommy is hammering and misses, she yells, "Ow!"
Mommy shakes her thumb, "Ugh."

"Does it really hurt?" Julia asks.
Mommy nods.
"Double ugh," Julia says.

But then Daniel says, "Fifty times ugh."